S0-DTB-867

Sleepy Sun

With love to my Princess, Brittany Priscilla ♥.

for Napa City-County Library

Mari Priscilla Hanson

Written by Mari Priscilla Hanson

Illustrated by Kathleen M. Hanson

ISBN:1-4196-7247-9
ISBN-13: 978-1419672477

The sun is getting sleepy

It had a busy day
Shining on the children playing
And swimming in the bay

The sun was in the sky
Where birds and airplanes flew
And with the farmers gathering corn
The beautiful sun rays grew

It shone on snow capped mountains
Where skiers *swooshed* downhill

And warmed a great big city
Where crowded streets would fill

cafe

Sunshine heated up the desert
Oh, what a hot and busy day!

It streamed through forest cabins

And to countries far away

Shimmering light in *your* backyard
Is what it liked the best!

It is growing very sleepy
Now it's settling down to rest

The sun is getting sleepy
It had a busy day
Just like you, My Little Child,
With all your busy play

We'll watch the sun one minute
As it lowers with a wink
It paints the sky with beauty
Orange and yellow hues with pink

It's time to go to sleep now
The stars are shining bright
It will see you in the morning
Goodnight, Sweet Child, goodnight

About the Author: **Mari Priscilla Hanson**

Photo/ Andrew Grant

Mari Priscilla Hanson first discovered her love for writing stories as a very young child, blending a lively imagination with a quick sense of humor. She now finds daily inspiration as the mother of her own beautiful and creative daughter, Brittany. In addition to writing professionally, Mari has worked in the vacation real estate industry in the United States and internationally. She holds a degree from Gonzaga University in Political Science.

For more information on Mari, or *Sleepy Sun*, go to: www.MariPriscillaHanson.com

About the Illustrator: **Kathleen M. Hanson**

Kathleen M. Hanson chose acrylic paint to showcase illustrations in this full color picture book, *Sleepy Sun*. Kathleen is well known for her Caribbean themed paintings, having lived in the islands for several years. Kathleen currently lives in Northern Arizona, and is an avid world traveler.